For Kevin, Noah and Sophie – my love, my soul, my spirit

Kane Miller, A Division of EDC Publishing

Text and illustrations copyright © Michelle Nelson-Schmidt 2011

For information contact:
Kane Miller, A Division of EDC Publishing
PO Box 470663
Tulsa, OK 74147-0663
www.kanemiller.com
www.edcpub.com
www.usbornebooksandmore.com

Library of Congress Control Number: 2010941501

Manufactured by Regent Publishing Services, Hong Kong
Printed April 2011 in ShenZhen, Guangdong, China

1 2 3 4 5 6 7 8 9 10

ISBN: 978-1-61067-041-8

Dogs, Dogs!

Michelle Nelson-Schmidt

Kane Miller
A DIVISION OF EDC PUBLISHING

Dogs, dogs, are everywhere.
Look at all the dogs out there!

fast

Fast dog, fast dog, in such a chase.
I think you must be in some big race!

dog

little

Little dog, little dog, oh, so cute.
Take a ride in my rain boot!

dog

fat

Fat dog, fat dog, just look at you eat.
I think you've had too many treats!

dog

sad

Sad dog, sad dog, you seem so glum.
Let's go play with your favorite chum!

dog

pretty

Pretty dog, pretty dog, what a fancy bow.
You're ready to win ribbons at a show!

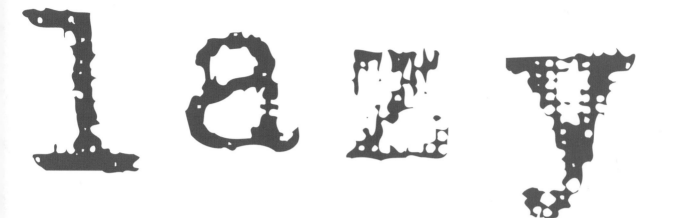

lazy

Lazy dog, lazy dog, just lying still.
Not even this ball gives you a thrill?

dog

happy

Happy dog, happy dog, why do you bark?
It must be because we're going to the park!

dog

scared

Scared dog, scared dog, shivering under the rug.
It's OK; you just need a great big hug!

dog

DiRTY

Dirty dog, dirty dog, digging lots.
No bones are hiding in the flower pots!

dog

shaggy

Shaggy dog, shaggy dog, with so much hair.
Do you really have eyes under there?

dog

stubborn

Stubborn dog, stubborn dog, pulling away.
There's just a little rain today!

dog

big

Big dog, big dog, what a giant you are.
You're almost as big as a little car!

dog

dogs, dogs!

Little girl, little boy,
reading this book.

Which dog are you like?
Take a look!

dogs, dogs!

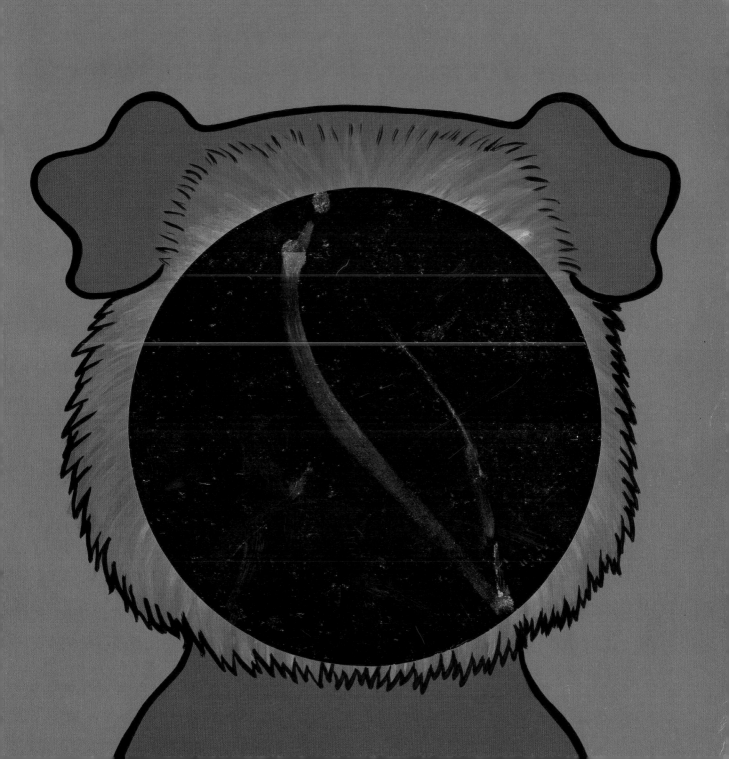

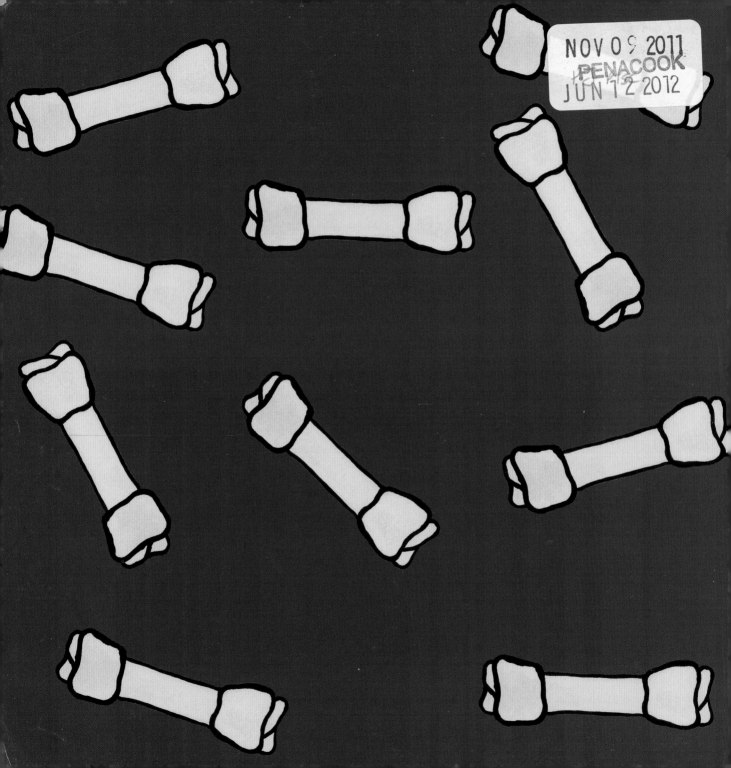